Also by Jean Ure

Sandy Simmons

☆ SAVES THE DAY! ☆

Jean Ure

Illustrated by Peter Kavanagh

 ORCHARD BOOKS

For Clare with love
P.K.

ORCHARD BOOKS
96 Leonard Street, London EC2A 4XD
Orchard Books Australia
14 Mars Road, Lane Cove, NSW 2066
First published in Great Britain in 1999
First paperback edition 2000
Text © Jean Ure, 1999
Illustrations © Peter Kavanagh, 1999
The rights of Jean Ure to be identified as the author
and Peter Kavanagh as the illustrator of this work
have been asserted by them in accordance with the
Copyright, Designs and Patents Act, 1988.
A CIP catalogue record for this book is available
from the British Library.
1 86039 567 8 (hbk)
1 84121 019 6 (pbk)
1 3 5 7 9 10 8 6 4 2 (hbk)
1 3 5 7 9 10 8 6 4 2 (pbk)
Printed in Great Britain

CONTENTS

Chapter one

Me and my best friend Sasha were talking on the telephone. "Shall I tell you who was really good?" said Sasha. "Really, *really* good?"

We were discussing the dress rehearsal of a play that was being put on by the senior pupils at Starlight, which is our stage school. All of us juniors had been allowed to go and watch.

"That girl with the red hair," said Sasha. "Millie Murphy. She was *really* good."

"Oh, she *was*," I agreed. "She was absolutely *brilliant*."

Somewhere near my left ear I heard this disgusting noise, like a person being sick. It was my brother Thomas pretending to throw up. I turned my back on him.

"The way she did that bit where she had to fall down the stairs," said Sasha.

"I *know*!" I said. "I nearly *died*!"

"I really thought she'd gone and slipped."

"Me too! I couldn't *believe* it."

Thomas had come dancing round to the front of me. He stood there pulling stupid faces and making "hurry-up" movements with his hands. I did my best to ignore him.

"They *say*," said Sasha, "that lots of top agents and directors are coming to the performance."

"*No?*" I shrieked.

"It's what I heard," said Sasha.

Thomas swooshed at me with his hands. I knew he wanted me to get off the phone, but why should I? I had as much right to talk to people as he did. He could wait!

"Imagine," sighed Sasha, "if one of them saw us selling programmes and said, 'That's the girl I want to star in my next big Hollywood movie.'"

"Oh, *wow!*" I did a mock swoon, with the telephone pressed against my forehead. Thomas instantly made a swipe at it, but I kicked at him and he backed off. "I'm fainting just at the thought of it!"

"You're what?" squeaked Sasha.

I clamped the telephone back to my ear. "I'm f-f-f-f-fainting!"

"STUPID LUVVIES!" roared Thomas.

Sasha giggled. "What was that?"

"Only my idiotic brother," I said.

Thomas gave me this really *filthy* look and went tearing out of the room, slamming the door behind him.

"What's his problem?" said Sasha.

"I don't know. Just because he wants to use the telephone, I expect. He's one big pain, he—" I broke off as the door banged back open and Thomas reappeared. He had Mum with him.

"Uh-oh!" I said. "The heavy mob!"

"Sandy!" Mum pointed crossly at her watch. "Get off the telephone!"

"Got to go," I said. "Chow!"

'Chow' was what we were saying that

term; I don't know why. Maybe next term it would be 'Afghan hound' or 'Yorkie'. We go through these phases.

"Luvvy!" hissed Thomas.

"Bore," I said.

"Just be quiet," said Mum. "You've been on that phone for nearly three-quarters of an hour!"

"I was talking to Sasha," I said.

"Talking to Sasha? But you see her every day! What on earth do you find to talk about?"

"Nothing," said Thomas. "It's all froth and bubble." He snatched up the telephone. "What I have to discuss is *important.*"

"Why?" I said, "Who are you ringing? The Prime Minister?"

"Sandy." Mum took my arm and moved me off towards the door. "Leave Thomas alone. He wants to talk to Nicky. It's serious."

Serious. Huh! Nicky Mann is this itty squitty boy in Thomas's class at school. He's also Thomas's best friend, like Sash is mine.

"Have they had a row?" I said. Me and Sasha never have rows. Other people do, but not us. On the other hand, if I was Thomas's friend I would probably have rows with him all the time, practically. He is the most inFURIATING person.

"I suppose they've fallen out," I said.

Mum said no, they hadn't fallen out, but it was something very important.

"It's important what me and Sash were talking about!" I said. "We were saying what we thought of the show. *That's* important, if I'm going to be an actress."

Which I am! SANDY SIMMONS, STAR OF STAGE AND SCREEN. That's what I'm going to be.

"We have to develop our critical faculties," I said.

"Yes, I'm sure," agreed Mum, pushing me into the kitchen. "But Thomas is worried about the cats."

"*Our* cats?" I said. "What's wrong with them?"

They were sitting on the table in two furry heaps. A black heap (Sheba) and a fat heap (Bunter). They looked OK to me.

Mum explained that it wasn't our cats, it was the cats at Cats' Cottage.

"Oh!" I began to understand.

Cats' Cottage is a cat sanctuary run by

Nicky's mum. It's where our two came from. Thomas helps out there as much as he can. He's crazy about cats. About any sort of animal. We all are, in our family, but Thomas especially. He's going to be a vet when he grows up. (He's amazingly clever, I have to admit it.)

"They're not short of money again?" I said.

"I'm afraid they are," said Mum. "And, this time, it's for real. They might even have to close."

"But what about the cats?" I said.

There are dozens of cats at Cats' Cottage. Big cats, small cats, sick cats, healthy cats. Cats of all kinds: some of them are blind, or deaf, or have only three legs because of accidents. Some of them have been ill-treated or abandoned. Some are just old. Nicky's mum takes them all in.

"Where would they go?" I wailed.

"Well, that's the problem," said Mum. "There's a real fear they'd have to be put down."

I stared at her in horror. Put down all those poor trusting moggies? That would be like murder!

"Now you can see why Thomas is so worried," said Mum.

I was worried too! Why hadn't someone told me?

Thomas came back into the kitchen. He picked up Sheba and buried his face in her fur.

"So what's happening?" said Mum.

"Got one more week."

"For what?" I said.

"For raising money!" shouted Thomas.

"You don't have to *yell*," I told him. "Why didn't you say anything to me?"

"What's the point? You're not interested in anything except your stupid acting! It's all you ever talk about."

"Hush now," said Mum. "Getting cross isn't going to solve anything."

"That's *right*," I said. "We have to think about the cats."

"I've been thinking about them!" roared Thomas. "While you've been messing around *acting*, I've been doing things!"

"What sort of things?" I said. "Jumble sales? Car boot sales?"

"We've done all that!"

"They've really been trying," said Mum. "You've got another jumble sale tomorrow, haven't you, Thomas?"

Thomas nodded.

"And a big fair in St Andrew's hall next Saturday. They're doing as much as they possibly can."

"Maybe you'd like me to help," I said.

I said it really politely. Really *graciously*. He was lucky I said it at all, considering how horrid he'd been. But I was thinking of the cats.

"If there's anything I can do, just let me know," I said.

"You?" said Thomas. "What could you do?" He rushed to the door. "Stupid luvvy!"

Mum said I had to forgive him because he was upset, but I made a vow it was the last time *I* would offer to help.

Chapter two

Next day was Saturday. We don't usually go in to school on a Saturday; just sometimes, like if we have a special rehearsal. But today was when the Upper School were putting on their show, and some of us had been chosen to be ushers.

Being an usher is quite important. It means saying hello to people when they arrive, and offering to take their coats, and asking them if they'd like a programme, and showing them to their seats.

Miss Todd, who is Head of Theatre

Studies, told us that we were "representing the school".

"So I want your best manners, please! A smile at all times. You are there to make people feel welcome."

I would like to say that I had been chosen because I was Especially Promising. I mean, I am especially promising. You Bet! I am going to be a ★S★T★A★R★. (This is not boasting: it is my aim in life.)

But in fact all that happened was that Miss Todd put everyone's name into a box and the first six she picked were the ones that got to be ushers. So it was just luck, really.

But, as Sasha says, you need a bit of luck if you are going to get anywhere.

"There are some people that are lucky, and some that aren't. It's as simple as that."

Our two special friends, Dell and Rosa, hadn't been lucky. They were dead envious of me and Sasha, but not jealous, because of being our friends.

"Friends don't get jealous," said Rosa. "They just want to scratch your eyes out!" And she made scratching motions with her fingers, but we knew she was only joking.

We had to be in school by two o'clock. Miss Todd said that we were to wear school uniform, which was a pity as it meant I couldn't get dressed up and impress agents.

I said this to Mum and she laughed and said, "Which agents?"

"Agents that might be there to watch the show," I told her.

"What makes you think they'd be impressed? They're not there to look at you!"

I said, "*Mum!* They might catch sight of me and get me a part in a Hollywood movie!"

"What as?" said Thomas. "A tomato?"

Stupid smart mouth! He only said it because of our school uniforms being bright red.

"You wait till I'm a big star," I said. "I'll be able to give huge megabuck cheques to people like Nicky's mum to help the cats!"

"Be too late by then," muttered Thomas. He choked. "They'll all have been killed!"

"Oh, Thomas!" Mum went chasing after him. "Don't be like that! You've got your jumble sale this afternoon, you've got the fair next weekend… Everyone's doing their very best!"

Everyone except me. I wasn't doing anything. But I'd offered! I wasn't going to offer again.

I flounced upstairs to the bathroom to wash my hair with some special Gleem shampoo that I'd bought. Even in school uniform and looking like a tomato I *might* just be noticed. You never know your luck!

Thomas was leaving the house at the same time as me. He was going down the road to Nicky's: I was going up the road to the tube station, to meet Sash. We collided with each other at the front door.

"After *you*," I said.

"After *you*," said Thomas; and he made this grand gesture like he was Sir Walter Raleigh

laying down his cloak for Queen Elizabeth to trample over. "You're the big star," he said, "after all."

"Oh, get on, the pair of you!" said Dad. He'd heard from Mum the way we'd been pecking at each other.

"Yes, you'd better shift," said Thomas, "or all the other luvvies will get there first and be spotted before you are."

"Thomas! Button it," said Dad.

At least Dad is on my side. *Sometimes.*

Mum came to see us off. To Thomas she said, "Good luck!" To me she just said, "Have fun!" She didn't take it seriously, the idea that I could end up in a Hollywood movie.

The other people who were ushers were:

✬ Barry Brown, who has a head like a turnip but is funny

✡ Buster Wells, who is going to grow into a hunk (my Auntie Lily says so)

✡ Starlotta Sharman, who is one big pain and

✡ Petal Lovejoy, who is probably going to go bald if she doesn't stop messing with her hair and dyeing it different colours (it was all pink and frizzy like candy floss just at the moment).

We all gathered in the Green Room, which is like a sort of actors' lounge, waiting for Miss Todd to come and inspect us and dish out some programmes.

"Hey, Sandy! Tell them what your brother called you," said Sash.

"He called me a stupid luvvy," I said. "He's always doing it. He thinks actors are just fribbles."

"I'd like to meet your brother," said Buster.

"No, you wouldn't," I said. "You'd end up wanting to bash him."

"It must be so-o-o-o difficult for you," gushed Starlotta. "I mean, coming from a family without any theatrical connections. I'm so lucky that way."

Starlotta has this gross fat uncle that's on the telly. He's OK really, I guess; it's just that we get bored to death hearing about him all the time.

Anyway, I do have theatrical connections. I have my Auntie Lily. I said so to Starlotta.

"Oh, but yes! Of course!" Starlotta smiled sweetly. "Your Auntie Lily! I was forgetting

Auntie Lily. She used to be a pupil here, didn't she? Way back in...when was it? The turn of the century?"

I felt my cheeks growing red and angry. I hate it when people make fun of Auntie Lily. She is Mum's cousin and a bit – well – peculiar, I suppose. Like she wears these really odd clothes that she gets from Oxfam shops. (She once turned up in a dress made out of *feathers*!) And she keeps her money in her knickers so that nobody can steal it. She is also quite old. But not as old as the turn of the century!

"Did your Auntie Lily ever actually do anything?" said Petal.

"Yes," I said. "She was leading lady with the Penzance Players."

There was a silence.

"Where's Penzance?" said Barry.

"Cornwall!" I snapped. Dumb turnip head.

"Cornwall." Starlotta nodded kindly. "Well, I suppose everyone has to start somewhere. Personally I'm going straight into television."

"Oh, really?" I said. "I'm going to go into films."

I looked at myself in the Green Room mirror. I have what my mum describes as a cheeky sort of face. I could play one of those parts where a child is kidnapped by a criminal and they go off together and the child gives the criminal what for and keeps telling him off and bossing him and in the end they become good friends and we discover the criminal isn't so bad after all. That is the sort of part I'd be good at. I wouldn't want to play anything sloppy and slurpy.

"Hey!" said Sasha. "I only just noticed... You've washed your hair in something. It's all gleaming!"

"That's because I washed it in GLEEM. Gleem shampoo for really *gleeeeeeeeeemy* hair," I said, pretending to be someone in a TV commercial. "I did it in case there's any film directors around."

"Film directors!" Sasha gave an amused titter. "Film directors don't come to drama schools!"

"Well then, agents," I said.

"Agents come to the evening

performance," said Starlotta.

Me and Sash exchanged glances. Sash pulled a face. We wouldn't be there in the evening. The older ones were on duty then.

Bother, I thought. I'd gone and wasted money on special shampoo all for nothing!

"I expect I shall probably meet an agent or two," said Starlotta. She did a little twirl. "I'm coming with my uncle. He knows all the top people. He's promised to introduce me."

You see what I mean about Starlotta being a pain. Not just a pain, but a PAIN. One great big enormous mega-huge PAIN.

Sometimes I feel like strangling her.

I prayed that Thomas wouldn't ask me if I'd been spotted by anyone. I'd had enough sneering and jeering from Starlotta; I didn't want him starting in on me as well.

When I got home, however, I found the house sunk in deepest gloom.

"How did your jumble sale go?" I said brightly to Thomas. I just wanted to show him that I was interested and that I cared. "Did you make oodles of beautiful dosh?"

By way of reply Thomas snarled, "What's it to you?" and went banging out of the room. He was doing a lot of banging and barging just lately. *And* slamming of doors. Usually if we slam doors Mum tells us off. Well, she tells me off. She didn't say a word to Thomas.

"What happened?" I said.

Mum sighed. "I'm afraid it was a disaster. Hardly anybody turned up. They only made about fifty pounds."

"Isn't that enough?" It seemed quite a lot to me, but Mum shook her head.

"Nowhere near! They've got a vet's bill of two hundred. It's such a shame! Thomas and Nicky worked so hard."

I couldn't help feeling sorry for Thomas — I mean, he was still my brother, even if he had been mean to me — but I felt even more sorry for all the poor cats.

What was going to happen to them? I just couldn't bear to think of it!

33

Chapter three

In the middle of the night
I woke up with this incredibly
and utterly amazing brilliant
idea. Even though I say it
myself. It was a WINNER!

I was so excited I wanted to go bouncing
out of bed straightaway to call Sasha, only I
looked at my clock and it said half past four
and I thought maybe Sasha's mum and dad
mightn't like me ringing at half past four.
Sasha wouldn't mind. Not when she heard
my idea! But parents are strange.

I once woke my mum and dad to tell
them something Miss Todd had said to me

at school. She'd said I had the makings of a real comedian. "I can see you with your own television show one of these days!"

Well! I mean. You'd think any normal parents would instantly go whizzing downstairs for a bottle of champagne. A daughter with her own television show!

Instead, Dad just groaned and Mum said, "Go back to bed, Sandy. Tell us in the morning."

So I didn't ring Sasha. I lay there with this brilliant idea fizzing round my brain, and lots of other, littler ideas going off like firecrackers. Whoosh! Swish! Bang! I was glad when morning came, I can tell you.

As soon as breakfast was over, I asked Dad if I could borrow his mobile phone.

He said, "Why? What's wrong with the ordinary phone?"

"I want to call Sasha," I said. "I want to have a private conversation."

"She thinks anyone wants to listen to the stuff she yatters on about?" jeered Thomas.

"You did the other day," I said.

"I did not," said Thomas.

"You did so!"

"I over*heard*," said Thomas. "You can't help overhearing when a person shrieks all the time."

"I do n—"

"Oh, for heaven's sake!" said Dad. "Take the phone and go and shriek in your bedroom and give us all some peace."

Thomas smirked.

"Two little luvvies having secrets," he said.

I don't know whether all boys are horrid or whether it's just Thomas. I almost felt like giving the phone back to Dad and saying, "If that's how you feel, I won't bother!" But my idea was just *so* brilliant. And, anyway, it was for the cats. Not for Thomas.

Sasha agreed with me that my idea was brilliant. She said that I was a genius to have thought of it.

"Except that a week doesn't give us very much time," she said.

I said that was why I had rung her. "So we can get started."

"What, you mean like today?" said Sasha.

"Like *immediately*," I said.

"OK. So who do you reckon we should use?"

"Everybody that's willing!"

"Everybody in our class? Even Starlotta?"

I struggled for a moment, then said, "Yes. Even Starlotta." Starlotta's a pain but she is quite a good actress and has had lots of experience. Also, I reminded myself again, it was *for the cats.*

"What about boys?" said Sash.

I struggled a bit more. The trouble with boys is that they tend to take over. They talk in loud voices and won't let anyone else get a word in. And then, before you know it, they're in charge and telling everyone what to do.

I don't think they mean to. It's just something they can't seem to help.

But this was my idea and I didn't want anyone taking over.

"Maybe the boys won't want to," I said.

"But if they do—"

"Then I suppose we'll have to let them."

I am not sexist! No way! I just don't like being pushed around. But Barry and Buster aren't too bad; and it was for the cats.

Sasha and me talked for nearly an hour, then her mum yelled at her that her nan had arrived and she had to go.

"See you tomorrow!" she said. "We'll get people organised."

After Sasha had gone, I rang Rosa. When Rosa heard my idea she said, "Oh! A sort of musical."

"Sort of," I said.

"Like *Cats*."

"It's *for* cats," I said. "To stop them being killed."

"No! The show called *Cats*. Have you seen it?"

And then she starts off warbling at the other end of the line, because Rosa loves to sing – it's her great passion in life. She's only tiny, but she has this immensely enormous voice that can break glasses and make the floor shake. Once she starts you just can't stop her.

I stood there with Dad's mobile held at arm's length, waiting for the noise to die down. It's a bit shattering when it's going straight into your ear.

"We could do some numbers from it!" carolled Rosa, getting all excited.

"No," I said. "This is going to be *our* thing. Not something written by someone else."

"Oh." Rosa sounded disappointed. "How can we write a musical in one week?"

I said, "We're not going to write a musical! It's a *happening*."

"But don't I get to sing?" said Rosa anxiously.

"Only catty songs... Miaaaaaaow!" I yowled at her down the telephone. Bunter, who was curled up on my bed, stared at me in catty outrage. Maybe it was because I'd interrupted his sleep. Or maybe I was saying something rude in catty language!

Rosa heaved a sigh.

"You won't be getting the best out of me. I have to sing if I'm really going to come alive."

"You could always miaow a tune," I said.

And I started making cat sounds to the
tune of 'Old MacDonald Had a Farm'.

"*Meeow owee owee ow*
Meeow owee ow.
Meeow owee owee—"

"Stop!" shrieked
Rosa. "That's terrible!"
It's true that singing is
not my strongest point.
When I am a star with
my own telly show I shall sing funny songs
and make people laugh.

"Do some thinking," I told Rosa, and she
promised that she would.

Next I rang Dell. Dell is always very cool.
She never gets stage-fright, she never bawls
or yells.

She listened while my big idea, plus all the littler ones, came tumbling out of me, and then at the end she said, "Hm! Looks like we shall have to get our skates on."

That is what Miss Todd says when she wants us to hurry up. "Get your skates on, people!"

"Do you really think we can do it?" I asked Dell.

"Do anything if you put your mind to it," said Dell.

I began to feel a whole lot happier when Dell said that. After talking to Rosa I'd almost begun to get cold feet. Suppose everybody just wanted to do their own thing and nobody would co-operate and we all just ended up arguing? Then we'd really be like silly luvvies and I would feel so ashamed. All those poor darling cats would be killed and I wouldn't have done a thing to help save them!

I'd been talking to Dell for about half an hour when there was a rat-a-tat-tat on my bedroom door. I thought it was Thomas coming for Bunter so I yelled, "Go away! I'm having a private conversation!"

It wasn't Thomas. It was Dad. He opened the door and stuck his head round and said, "Stone me! You're not still on that phone?"

I didn't dare make any jokes about the heavy mob. Dad was definitely not looking pleased.

"I'd better go," I said to Dell.

"Yes, I think you had," said Dad. He held

out a hand for the telephone. "That's the
last time I trust you with this, young lady!
You brought this phone up here" – he
looked at his watch – "two and a
half hours ago!"

"I haven't been talking *all*
the time," I said.

"No? Well, we shall
see," said Dad, "when
the bill comes in."

He went on and on.
You'd think I'd committed some truly
hideous crime. All I'd been doing was just
trying to save some little cats' lives!

We sat down to dinner and Dad was still
going on. Grumbling to Mum about the
cost of telephone bills.

"Goodness knows who she's been calling!
New York, Sydney—"

"I don't know anyone in New York," I said. "And I don't know anyone called Sidney."

"All right, miss! That's enough smart mouth!" said Dad.

I looked at him, hurt. What had I said?

"Stupid luvvy!" jeered Thomas.

I was going to kick at him under the table, but I reminded myself just in time that he was upset about the cats. So I glared at him instead.

If he hadn't been so horrid to me I'd have told him about my brilliant idea and stopped him worrying. As it was, he would just have to *wait*!

Chapter four

Next day at break time, me and Sasha
gathered all our class together in the corner
of the playground
and told them my
idea for saving
the cats of Cats'
Cottage. Everyone

except Starlotta agreed that it was brilliant.

Starlotta just stood there pulling faces
and rolling her eyes and making like she
was so-o-o-o superior. Like she thought my
idea was really stupid and babyish and she
didn't want anything to do with it. So I
ignored her. She hates being ignored.

"First we've got to find out who wants to be in and who doesn't," I said.

"Hands up everyone who does," ordered Sasha.

All the girls put their hands up. Even, in the end, Starlotta! She heaved this big dramatic sigh and said, "Oh, I *suppose*...if it's for *cats*," and sort of drooped her arm over her head.

"Is that meant to be up or down?" said Sasha.

"Up!" snapped Starlotta.

I knew she couldn't bear to be left out!

Only two of the boys could do it, Barry Brown and Ahmed Khan. All the rest were playing football on Saturday afternoon. I was secretly a bit relieved about this, though naturally I didn't say so!

"Now we've got to decide who's going to be the lady who rescues the cats," I said.

Nobody wanted to be the lady who rescued the cats because everybody wanted to be cats. Rosa said that the tallest person should do it, and we all agreed. But we had *two* tallest people, Dell and Starlotta. It wasn't until we stood them back to back that we discovered Dell was taller than Starlotta by about a quarter of a millimetre. Starlotta immediately said that meant that Dell had to be the lady.

Then Sasha pointed out that Dell ought to be a cat because Dell *looks* like a cat, and this is perfectly true. Dell has this beautiful cat-shaped face with big wide-apart eyes and a little catlike nose. Starlotta has a *long* nose and a *long* face. She doesn't look in the least bit like a cat.

We wasted simply ages arguing about this, until at last I had another of my totally brilliant ideas and pointed out to Starlotta that the lady who rescued the cats would be the STAR PART.

I said, "You'll be the one who asks people for money."

So then she changed her mind and said OK, in that case she supposed she'd better do it. Making like she was the only one that possibly *could*, being so much better than the rest of us. But I didn't mind, if it kept her happy. After all, it was for the cats.

"Now what do we do?" said Petal.

I said, "Now we have to decide what sort of cats we're going to be."

"I'm going to be a tom-cat!" shouted Barry. "Big fierce tom-cat!"

Ahmed said that he was going to be a tom-cat, too. Being a tom-cat meant having punch-ups and chasing all the lady cats.

"Like this!"

Before I knew it, everyone was rushing about screaming and yowling and making catty sounds.

When I say everyone, I mean – well! I mean that I was doing it too. This is the sort of thing that happens when you have boys around. Everything gets all mad and noisy.

Suddenly, in this really loud, cross voice, Starlotta demanded, "Are we trying to rescue cats or are we just playing stupid games?"

"We're chasing women!" bawled Barry. He made a lunge at Rosa. Rosa screeched and fell over. Barry fell on top of her. Rosa giggled.

"You are all so *unprofessional!*" yelled Starlotta.

It was that that made us stop. I felt really ashamed. We were pupils at a famous stage school! We were supposed to be *serious*. Plus we had all those poor moggies depending on us to save them from a horrible death.

"Behaving like a bunch of five-year-olds," grumbled Starlotta. "If we're going to do this thing, then let's do it!"

Even Starlotta has her good points.

All that week we worked on my idea. We told Miss Todd what we were planning and she said we could use the gym for rehearsing in.

Everyone made up their own little cat story and their own little cat character to go with it. We were going to tell the stories just with dance steps and mime, except for Rosa who said she was going to sing a little kitty song, but that was all right. Rosa can sing in tune even without any music.

We all practised our cat make-up and made our own cats' tails to pin to the backs of our leotards. It's easy making a cat's tail! You just take a pair of old tights and cut off one leg and stuff it with something soft, like cotton wool, Then if you wriggle your bottom it swishes about just like a real tail!

Dell had a clever idea how to make paws.

She took another pair
of tights (old ones) and
cut off the feet, like this:

Then she sewed
bits of tape onto
them, like this:

Then she put
her hands into
them, like this:

And tied the tapes round her wrists
(remembering to tuck the ends in) and
there she was, with cats' paws!

From a distance it looked really good,
especially when she did catty
sort of things such as
rubbing her whiskers or
washing behind her ears.

Of course the boys said they couldn't do it.

"Can't sew," said Ahmed.

"Then it's time you learnt!" snapped Rosa.

"But it's girls' stuff," said Barry.

"So's this!" cried Rosa,
and she took hold of
him by both his ears
and stuck out her tongue.
In the end they said they'd
get their mums to do it. Pathetic.

Friday lunch time we held a dress rehearsal
in the gym. Miss Todd asked if she could
come and watch, so we were all on our best
behaviour. It went really well! Miss Todd
congratulated us. She said we were a credit
to the school. I was dead pleased until Petal
started off moaning and saying that a good
dress rehearsal meant a bad show.

"It means nothing of the kind!" snapped Starlotta. "That is just stupid superstition!"

One thing about Starlotta, she is a *real pro*. You have to admire her.

After school, me and Sasha stayed behind to do a poster. We used the computer (Miss Todd said we could) so that it would look professional and we could make a load of copies. We had decided to call ourselves The Luvvies. It was just a joke, really, to get our own back on Thomas.

The show was *supposed* to be called *Cats' Tales* but Sash went and spelt it *Cats' Tails* by mistake and I thought perhaps that was quite funny, so we left it.

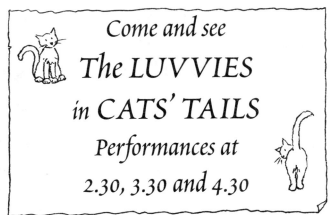

Come and see
The LUVVIES
in CATS' TAILS
Performances at
2.30, 3.30 and 4.30

Nicky's mum didn't seem one little bit grateful when I told her how we were going to make money to rescue the cats.

I said, "Me and my friends at stage school have made this show and we're going to come along to your fair and do it."

Well! You'd have thought she'd at least have said thank you. But she didn't. All she said was, "That's really nice of you, Sandy. You'll have to forgive me, I'm rushed off my feet." And that was it! She put the telephone down.

I'd been going to ask her not to say anything to Nicky (in case he told Thomas) only she didn't give me the chance. But somehow I didn't think she *would* say anything. I didn't think she was that interested.

She thought we were just a load of silly little kids, messing around. We would just have to prove her wrong!

When I got home I went up to my room to practise my cat dance just one more time.
I was a little street cat, playing in the sunshine.
I chased my tail,
I chased butterflies,
I had fun!
And then…

Then I ran into the road, and that was when all my troubles began.

The first part of my story was a happy one. I was still in the middle of it when Mum called to me to come and have tea, so I danced my way downstairs and along the hall. As I reached the kitchen the door

opened and Thomas
came out, carrying a
glass of orange.

Well! You can guess
what happened. That
orange went *everywhere.*
All down the wall, all over the carpet.

"You idiot!" yelled Thomas.

"Now what's happened?" cried Mum.

"The stupid luvvy's gone and spilt my
orange!" roared Thomas.

I just put my hands up like cat paws and
went, "Miaow!"

Thomas glowered at me. "What's
that supposed to be?"

"You'll see!" I said.

Next morning he was in for
a *real* surprise.

Oh, but so was I! When I woke up...

Chapter five

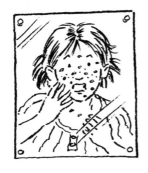

DISASTER! My cheeks
were all covered in
bright red spots!
"Mum!" I bawled.
"Mum!"

I went hurtling down
the stairs. Mum rushed out of the kitchen.

"Sandy! What on earth is the – oh, my
goodness! You've got the chicken pox!"

"I can't have!" I wailed.

I had things to do! I had cats to rescue.
I couldn't have the chicken pox!

"I'm afraid it looks as though you have,"
said Mum.

Thomas had come down and was skulking in the doorway.

"Chicken pox!" he sniggered.

He'd been horrid to me all week. *Really* horrid. It was because he thought I didn't care about the cats.

"It's not funny!" I said.

"I think it is," said Thomas. "You always wanted to be seen in a SPOTlight!"

Oh, ha ha! Very witty, I *don't* think.

"What a nuisance!" said Mum. "You'll have to be off school. And I'm sorry, Thomas, but you won't be able to go to the fair this afternoon."

"*Mum!*" We screamed it at her together.

"Not if you've got the chicken pox," said Mum.

"*I* haven't got it!" roared Thomas.

"It's only a matter of time. I can't let you go round infecting other people. Sandy! Get yourself back to bed. I'd better call the doctor."

"But I'm not *ill*," I said. "I feel perfectly all right!"

"That's funny," said Mum. She put a hand on my forehead. "You don't seem to have a temperature. And those spots…" She peered at them more closely.

"Hm!" she said. "That's odd!"

"W-what's odd?" I said.

"Come over here," said Mum.

She marched me across to the sink. Before I could stop her she was scrubbing away at my cheeks as hard as she could go

 with a scrubbing brush and soap.

"Ow! Ouch! Ouch!" I wriggled like mad, but Mum held me in a firm grasp.

"There!" she said. "That's better! Still a bit pink, but I think we can safely say it's not chicken pox."

"So w-what is it?" I stammered. I rubbed my hands over my face. It was all zingy and sizzling from where Mum had scrubbed at it. It could be something *fatal.* "What is it?" I screeched.

"I'm not quite sure," said Mum. "I wonder if your brother might know?"

"*Thomas!*"

I cornered him in the bathroom. I threatened to spray him all over with Dad's shaving foam if he didn't come clean.

"It was a joke!" he said. "It was a joke!"

That *disgusting* boy. He had crept into my room at dead of night and dribbled beetroot juice on me. I *hate* beetroot!

"You're such an idiot!" I yelled. "Mum might have made us both stay indoors!"

I'd been going to tell him about *Cats' Tails*, but now I decided not to. He was going to be the VERY LAST PERSON to know about it.

The fair started at two o'clock that afternoon. Thomas was going to get there early, so he could help people set up their stalls. Me and Sash were going to get there early, too. We wanted to pin up our posters and find ourselves a little corner. We had to get there before Thomas!

"Where are you going?" he said when he

saw me with my coat on.

"Going round to Sasha's," I said. "We have things to do. Far more important than your silly old fair!"

I know it was mean of me, but there are times when he just gets me so *mad.*

Sasha only lives five minutes away. I was round there in a flash.

"Quick!" I panted when Sasha came to the door. "We've got to get there before Thomas!"

We crammed a bag with our costumes and make-up, snatched the posters and ran. We were lucky! Nicky's mum was there, but Thomas hadn't arrived. And Nicky was down the far end of the hall and didn't see us. We were still a secret!

Nicky's mum was really surprised when she saw our posters. It was like all of a sudden she realised that we weren't just silly little kids. We were *serious*.

"My goodness!" she said. "This is most impressive!"

"We did it on the computer," said Sasha.

"We want to make loads of money for you," I said.

"Well! Where are we going to put you? I know!" She clapped her hands. "There's a little stage up there. Would that do?"

A stage! Sasha and me looked at each other. A real stage!

"It's only very tiny," said Nicky's mum.

"It's only a tiny show," said Sasha earnestly.

"But it is *professional*," I assured her.

Nicky's mum was right about the stage: it was *really* tiny.

"But kind of cute," said Sasha.

"And it's got curtains," I said.

We went back into the hall with our posters and some Blu-tak that we'd bought and we stuck posters absolutely everywhere. We stuck them on the curtains, we stuck them on the walls, we stuck them on the doors. We even stuck them in the toilets!

On our way back to the stage we bumped into Thomas. He said, "Oh, so you got here. You're far too early. We haven't opened yet." And then he caught sight of one of our posters and his jaw dropped. He said, "What's that?"

Me and Sasha studied it.

"Dunno," I said.

"Dunno," said Sasha.

Thomas narrowed his eyes. "Are you up to something?"

"What, *us?*" said Sasha. And we giggled and linked arms and went strolling off.

We'd told all the others to be there at two o'clock, so as soon as the doors opened we went and stood at the entrance and whispered, "On stage!" each time someone arrived.

Everyone turned up on time, because that is what they teach us at Starlight. "You must never, ever be late for a professional engagement." If we were, Miss Todd would put a black mark against our name. Three black marks and you're in trouble. Dead

trouble. It means you're not sent for any
more auditions for the rest of the term, and
if you still don't mend your ways you get
THROWN OUT.

It makes me go like jelly just to think of it!

When everybody had arrived, me and
Sash went backstage to get into our
costumes and put our make-up on. All the
others were already in their costumes. They
had travelled in them! But
they all carried their tails
except for Rosa, who trailed
hers behind her, sticking out
of her coat. It looked
really odd! But
Rosa doesn't care.
She never cares
about things
like that.

"If people want to stare, let them stare," she says.

Thomas stared like mad! His eyes were practically on stalks as Rosa and her tail went swishing down the hall.

Promptly at two thirty, Starlotta walked out between the curtains and blew on a trumpet that she had borrowed from her brother. Starlotta can't actually play the trumpet. All she can do is make loud braying noises.

"Parp p-p-parp PARP."

At least it attracted people's attention! Everyone fell silent and turned towards the stage.

"Ladies and gentlemen," announced Starlotta. "We proudly present...The Luvvies, in *Cats' Tails*!"

Then two of us whisked back the curtains

and the show began.

We came on in turns, to tell our stories. We were old cats, young cats, happy cats, sad  cats: cats that were lost, cats that were sick, cats that had been run over.

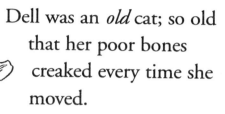

Dell was an *old* cat; so old that her poor bones creaked every time she moved.

Rosa was a singing cat, trilling her catty songs – until some cruel person chucked a stone at her and broke her leg.

Petal was a lost cat. She miaowed most piteously. Her heartless owners had moved away and left her behind.

Barry was a tom-cat who had been in a fight with a savage dog. Ahmed was attacked by a gang of bullies. Tiffany was starving.

I was a happy cat, playing in the sunshine. But I didn't look where I was going, and I ran in front of a car and got knocked down. Nobody bothered to stop and see if I was hurt. They just left me there, in the gutter.

By the end, the stage was full of sad little heaps. Poor little lost kitty cats, crouched in their corners. No one to love us, no one to take care of us.

And then the beautiful rescue lady arrived! She saw us all and she called to us, and one by one we crept up to her. She stroked us and petted us and gave us food and lovely warm beds. And we all started purring and rubbing against her to show how grateful we were.

But, oh, the money ran out! The rescue lady opened her purse and shook it, and it was empty. And we all went "Miaow!" and stretched out our paws, and the rescue lady showed her empty purse to the audience and said, "What am I to do? If someone doesn't help me, all these poor cats will starve!"

And we all looked as sad as we could and went "Miaaaaaow!" in our most pathetic

voices. And the rescue lady walked forward and held out her purse to the audience.

I have to tell you that it was a BIG purse. A *really* big purse. It was an old handbag belonging to Starlotta's gran and it was the size of a suitcase, practically!

Guess what? The audience almost filled it! One lady gave us a twenty pound note! Another lady gave us a cheque. When we looked at it later we found that it was for ONE HUNDRED POUNDS!!!

Everyone clapped and clapped and we all made little catty bows and rubbed our ears and our whiskers and set up a really loud purring.

The best moment of all was when we poured the money into a carrier bag and gave it to Nicky's mum. She cried. "Oh, I don't know what to say! This is so marvellous! I can't believe it!"

We couldn't quite believe it, either. We'd hoped to make a lot of money, but we hadn't expected twenty pound notes and a cheque for one hundred pounds!

We did two more performances, and after each one the big purse was filled with money.

"Will the cats be safe now?" said Rosa anxiously.

Nicky's mum hugged us all, one after another, and said yes, the cats would be safe. "But maybe next year, if we do another fair, The Luvvies might come back again?"

We promised that we would.

That evening, after tea, Thomas came up to me, all bright red, and muttered, "Sorry I called you a stupid luvvy."

"That's all right," I told him. I mean, I could afford to be generous. I'd helped save the cats!

"I'll tell you what," said Thomas. "When I'm a vet and you're a big star, I'll be sure and tell everyone you're my sister."

"Hey! Wow! Gee whizz!" I said, and I did a pretend faint.

I would never admit it to Thomas, but it was quite the nicest thing he'd ever said to me!

About the Author

Jean Ure was still at school when she had her first novel published. She's written lots of books since then, including the *Woodside School* stories and, for older children, *Love is Forever*. As well as writing, Jean really LOVES drama, acting and the theatre! After finishing school, Jean went to The Webber-Douglas Academy and some of her ideas for the *Sandy Simmons* stories come from her experiences there. Jean now lives in Croydon with her husband, seven dogs and three cats.